I0621472

RIA VARGAS

Text Me When You're Dead

First published by Trunk Up Books 2025

Copyright © 2025 by Ria Vargas

This novel is entirely a work of fiction. The names, characters and incidents portrayed in it are the work of the author's imagination. Any resemblance to actual persons, living or dead, events or localities is entirely coincidental.

First edition

This book was professionally typeset on Reedsy.
Find out more at reedsy.com

Contents

Chapter 1

An insistent vibration thrums against my desk. Once, it would've sent my heart skipping, but now, it only leaves me tired.

I can't even imagine...

How are you?

I'm so sorry for your loss.

Or worse, the dreaded phone calls.

The office around me is too bright. Fluorescents hum overhead, casting everything in a sterile sort of haze. What I wouldn't give to be back at home, curled up on the couch. But bills don't wait for grief, and neither does rent. So here I am, back under these unforgiving lights, pretending to focus while my mind slips away.

My cell buzzes again, the screen lighting up to reveal the background image. A bar, somewhere downtown. Loud music, too loud to hear myself think. My drink sweating into my hand as Theo leaned close and whispered, his lips at my ear.

"Everything I want," he'd said, "is right here." Laughter and liquor lit up his eyes; they always did, when he got away with saying too much. Or too little. Sometimes it was hard to tell which. But that night was different.

Fifteen calls. I haven't checked since yesterday. Or was it the day before? I can't remember. My grip loosens as I swipe through the list, seeing the names but not really registering them. They don't matter. Sadness tears through my chest, sharp and fresh. I blink hard, forcing my eyes back to my computer. Cell formulas blur together, green and black bleeding into a confusion of words and numbers.

There's a rhythm to the tap-tap of keys around me, a chorus of muted office conversations. It should make me feel less alone. Instead, I'm achingly aware of how untethered I am. Someone laughs near the copier; someone else crinkles paper, leans back in a chair. Their noises cut in and out like a radio signal too weak to keep hold. I wonder how much they know.

The spreadsheet cell in front of me reads #REF! I don't bother stifling a frustrated sigh. Population data that doesn't exist or has been lost. I click back through the tabs, opening all the dead ends, double-checking. Triple-checking. Preferring the soothing certainty of numbers to…well, everything.

Maybe this is what grief is. Staring at a screen. Refreshing a formula. Hiding your hurt from your coworkers. I used to think I understood loss, but that was before Theo slipped away like smoke. *Who am I without him?*

A colleague stops by, hovering. They ask about a report, but I can't make out the words. The faint suggestion of sympathy registers on their face as I say I'll have it done, as I send them on their way. I wait until their footsteps retreat before pushing out my chair and heading down the hall to the break room.

I stare into my coffee. Bitter, black, undrinkable. Just like yesterday. Just like the day before. Cold light flickers against the too-white walls of the break room, the open space crowded with solitude. My pulse echoes through my ribs. I close my eyes and almost hear his voice through the hum of the fridge.

When I finally look up, she's there, Jessa, her red hair like a sunrise through a storm. She leans against the counter, arms crossed, that little wrinkle in her forehead that I know too well. She sees right through me. Always has.

"You know I'm here for you, right?" Her voice is soft, steady. The kind of steady that makes you feel like the floor's still there even when everything else is gone.

I nod. Of course I do.

"You don't have to pretend."

I shrug. "I'm not pretending."

Her mouth tightens—not judgment, not doubt. The quiet ache of someone who's trying to hold space without holding the pain.

"You can talk to me, Sloane."

I shift my weight, feigning interest in the wall. "I'm fine." The lie feels brittle in my throat. A shard of something I can't quite swallow.

She doesn't call me on it. But she doesn't let it go, either.

"You ever get the feeling," I say, the words surprising even me, "that the more you try to remember someone, the more they blur?"

She tilts her head. "Blur how?"

"Like…" I search for the right edge of it. "You remember what they meant, but not how they sounded. Or the way they moved. The little things. You press your fingers around the memory, but it keeps slipping away."

I pause. Then softer: "Sometimes I feel like I made parts of him up."

Jessa's expression changes—slightly, but it's enough. Her eyes go glassy for half a second before she blinks hard. She steps closer, sets her hand on mine. Warm, solid. Anchoring.

"You loved him," she says, the words low and full of heat. "That's the realest thing there is."

Something in my chest gives a little under the pressure.

Jessa glances toward the clock on the wall. "I should get back. Text me before you head out, yeah?"

I nod, but don't speak.

She walks out, and for a second, the room feels hollow without her in it.

Then I hear voices in the hallway—low at first. Muffled. But not for long.

"She needs to get over it already."

Zack.

I freeze.

"I'm sick of walking on eggshells just because she's the sad girlfriend."

Jessa's voice cuts through, sharp as snapped glass. "Wow. That's what you're going with? That's who you're choosing to be today?"

There's a pause, thick with tension.

Zack scoffs—thin and nasally. "I'm just saying what everyone else is thinking."

"No. You're saying the thing people are too *decent* to say out loud."

His voice sharpens. "You've been covering for her since she got back."

"It's been three weeks!" she hisses. Her words hang there, suspended, before their argument picks back ups, their muffled voices turning to static.

Has it really been that long?

Then come the footsteps—hers first. I can picture her now, weaving through the narrow maze of desks and shared screens, eyes locked forward, jaw tight.

Zack's retreat is slower. Less certain. His footsteps drag, punctuated by the occasional squeak of cheap office flooring underfoot as he heads the other way.

Outside the breakroom, the office hum returns: keyboards clicking, phones ringing, someone laughing too loudly across the bullpen. But it all sounds far away.

I pull my phone out, clear the swarm of notifications, and open my text thread with Theo. For a while, I scroll through the messages, losing myself in the memories. All the plans we made, the promises. The last text is from me, unanswered. At the time, I thought he was angry or upset with me. Even now, a pang of guilt shoots through my veins.

Get over it. Zack's voice echoed.

The words rise up inside me like a current. Cold and certain.

I won't.

Chapter 2

The clock ticks past five, and I close my laptop on an ocean of emails. I'll be expected to swim through them tomorrow, but that's a problem for then. When did every minute start to feel like drowning? I rub my eyes and lean back in my chair. Nobody's left in the office to notice me zoning out again, and that's a relief in itself. I can't stand the concerned glances, the thinly veiled sympathy. They mean well, but they don't know how heavy this grief feels. How can they? How can anyone?

At work, I hear the whispers. Like today, when I pretended not to notice how quiet they got when I walked in.

"At least she's back."

"At least she's here."

"At least…"

They trailed off. They think I'm unstable, not bouncing back fast enough. Zack's comments only confirmed what I already suspected. A heavy sigh leaves my chest as I shut my laptop. The air feels stifling even though I'm alone.

This place is a tomb.

I pack up my things, tossing them into my bag. There was a time when I'd arrange every item before heading out, a ritual of organization to clear my mind. *Sloane used to be meticulous,* I imagine them saying. *Sloane used to have it all together.* That was before. Now, everything blends together, and nothing matters. I press my lips into a thin line, swallowing back the bitterness.

At least…

The world spins as I stand, vertigo sweeping over me. My grip tightens on the edge of the desk, knuckles pale and strained. It passes, but the nausea doesn't. That hangs on like an unwanted companion, stubborn and unrelenting. I suck in a long, slow breath, release it like I'm deflating. Three seconds in, six seconds out, a therapist once taught me.

My phone vibrates, and my pulse spikes with sudden urgency. My mother or Jessa? Both have been hovering, alternating shifts. When I check the screen, disappointment tightens my throat. A low battery alert. As if to mock me, it buzzes again a second later: Five new emails. I shove the phone back into my pocket and run a hand through my hair, freeing it from today's confines.

I shrug on my coat and head to the door, shivering in the chill that permeates my bones despite the fabric. Jessa asked if I wanted company, but I told her no. She didn't fight me on it. She never does anymore, and that only makes me feel worse. Like she's given up too, resigned to this gray version of her friend. Resigned to the ghost that's moving into the space Sloane used to fill.

Breathe in. Breathe out.

God, I'm exhausted.

I move like a wind-up toy again, each step mechanical and deliberate as I spiral down flight after flight. The chill follows me into the night. As I fumble with the lock on my bike, I pause, hope stuttering in my chest. Maybe Jessa changed her mind. Maybe she'll be waiting at my place with ice cream and bad movies, ready to distract me until it feels okay to breathe again. Ready to stay as long as it takes.

And maybe I won't be alone after all.

The first few blocks fly by in a haze, and I wonder if I'm dreaming, pedaling through endless memories. I push myself faster, lungs screaming, legs burning, the pain a welcome distraction from the hollowness in my chest.

A man's body was found at the base of the cliffs, the newspaper said. No identification. Only a description: mid-thirties, blue eyes, dark hair. The report was weeks ago, but it lives in me now. I force air into my lungs as I turn the corner, trying not to see the diner where we used to eat breakfast every Saturday. I picture him on the patio, hands wrapped around a coffee cup, smiling like he knows I'm thinking about him, even though I'm blocks away. "Eggs and toast?" he'd text. I'd laugh, despite myself, always responding with the same lie.

"On my way."

I blink away tears, wiping them with the back of my hand before they have a chance to fall. My breath is ragged and uneven, and I push myself faster, desperate to outrun the pain.

My legs feel heavy, but I keep moving, pressing harder against the pedals, steering recklessly through intersections, through time. I coast past the park where we spent our last sunny afternoon. It's empty now, cold and barren, no hint of warmth or promise. The trees stand bare, like they're mocking me with their emptiness.

The wind bites at my cheeks and they sting. My mind loops back to the call. "I'm so sorry." the detective had said. Words I'm too familiar with now. That was it. A phone call, a few short sentences, and then he was gone. Theo was dead, and there was nothing left to say. Nothing left to hold on to.

How long until the pain disappears? How long until I can think about him without this crushing sense of loss, without the shame that bleeds into everything? How long until I can pretend I'm okay?

My lungs are on fire, but I push through it, push through the empty streets, push through the memories that drown me as I sink deeper into grief. I just need to get home before I break.

* * *

My hands tremble as I fit the key into the lock. It sticks, and I curse under my breath. I'm about to retreat to the silence inside, to let it swallow me whole, when my phone buzzes like an angry wasp in my pocket. I grit my teeth, irritated at another check-in from Jessa or my mother or anyone who thinks their concern can fill this void. But it's not them. It's not who I expect at all.

I stare at the screen, my heart pounding out a frantic rhythm. I read the words but can't process them, can't connect them to anything that makes sense. They blur into meaninglessness.

I'm sorry. I love you more than you know.

They stay there, stubborn and impossible, defying my disbelief. My first thought is a mistake. Wrong number. Autocorrect. Some glitch. But no. The number is his. *His* number.

I press my thumb to the screen, hesitating. Could it be a prank? Someone found his phone, decided to mess with me? But the phrasing... it feels personal. Why would someone say that? What would they gain?

My breath catches and holds, my entire world teetering on the edge of this one impossible message. Theo's dead. There was a call... I'm sure of it, but now I'm not sure of anything.

It's a prank, it has to be. But who would be this cruel? I read the message again, then a third time, then again and again until the words are a chant, a mantra that makes less sense every time I see them.

"I'm sorry."

He's alive?

"I love you more than you know."

I can't breathe.

My phone slips from my grip and clatters against the concrete. I reach for it, the movement clumsy and desperate. My heart is a wild thing in my chest, feral and panicked and out of control.

I shove the key into the lock, my motions frantic and unsteady. The door swings open, and I collapse inside, the phone still clenched in my fist. I clutch it to my chest like a lifeline. Or a time bomb.

I don't understand.

I unlock my phone with shaking hands and tap the message, opening it, reading it again and again. It doesn't change. It doesn't vanish or glitch. It's not imagined.

Hope burns hot and sudden in my chest, a flicker of something dangerous and bright. I let it linger for one reckless moment, then snuff it out before it can take hold.

It's not Theo. This is a lie. A cruel, ugly joke.

I don't know how long I sit there, how long I let the chaos swirl around me, how long I try to convince myself it's not real. A second ticks by, then another. I curl up on the floor, the phone pressed to my heart, and I let the tears come. They spill over, unchecked, unrelenting, until I can't tell where the relief begins and the panic ends.

It's the worst kind of hope, fragile and thrilling and a breath away from heartbreak. I cling to it, clutching it close, letting it fill the spaces that felt so empty. He's alive. He's alive. I want to believe. I want to believe so badly it hurts. I've missed him so much. So much more than I thought I could.

I imagine Theo, smug grin on his face, like he got me again, like it was all a game. I hear his voice, calm and confident, the way it always was when he knew more than he let on. "I'm sorry, Sloane," he'd say, and I'd throw my arms around him and never let go. I want to believe in that, want to believe it's him. I breathe in the possibility, reckless and bright. But doubt is a slow poison. It creeps into the edges, sinks its claws in deep.

He's gone.

The contradiction is a knot in my chest I can't unravel. If it's a scam, what's the endgame? If it's a trick, who benefits? If it's a joke, where's the punchline? If it's someone else, if it's someone pretending, what do they get out of it?

It has to be him.

…Doesn't it?

I type a single, solitary question mark. It's all I can manage. I press send.

I need to find out who's doing this. And if it's him—I need to know why.

The screen stares back at me, blank and expectant. My heart is a drum in my chest, loud and fast and impossible to ignore. I wait.

Three dots appear.

Then they freeze and vanish.

Chapter 3

Morning comes too fast. I didn't sleep—not really. I kept checking my phone like something might change, like the message might disappear or those three dots might come back.

They didn't.

I told myself I wouldn't think about it today. Not until I had more to go on. But it's still there, lodged behind my ribs like a bruise I keep pressing.

The stack of mail taunts me from the counter.

I've circled it all morning, picking up coffee cups and wiping crumbs off the stovetop just to avoid looking at it directly. Like if I stare too long, the wrong kind of memory might catch my eye and pull me under.

It's just mail. A few weeks' worth of paper ghosts—junk ads, bills, pre-approved nonsense—but it's also the last trace of Theo's life that feels unfinished. I should've tossed it already. Every time I walked past it, I told myself next time. After I've slept. After I've eaten. After the grief has become something quieter. But it hasn't.

I pull the pile toward me, thumbing through it. A gas bill. A medical flyer. A grocery store loyalty card addressed to THEO HARRIS in all-caps, the kind of font that doesn't know he's dead.

He didn't technically live here, but some would argue that his keys, toothbrush, and mess would say otherwise. So when he left for that hiking trip, I grabbed his mail without thinking. That's what you do when someone else's life folds into yours. Seamless. I didn't think it'd be the last time…

Sobs wrack my body, and I know I must look pathetic.

It's just mail. Junk. Paper. Pull yourself together!

Maybe part of me thought if I left it there long enough, it might start to mean something. Like he'd come back and say, *God, you kept this?* and I'd roll my eyes and say, *Well, I didn't want to throw out your electric bill.* And he'd smirk. Call me sentimental.

I reluctantly set to work, the minutes passing like hours. The piles shrink and just when I've hit a groove, a padded envelope catches my eye. It's addressed to neither of us. It's for Marcus Chen.

I blink, confused for a moment. Then it clicks. The envelope must've gotten mixed in, maybe when Theo grabbed both stacks from their mailbox and dumped them on my counter without looking. Or perhaps I had when I fetched the mail for him. It didn't matter.

I pull out my cell and scroll to the contact Theo once begrudgingly saved. Marcus was polite, soft-spoken. The opposite of Theo in so many ways.

I press call. My pulse quickens with every ring, but then it clicks over to voicemail. The tone is surprisingly formal, but there's no mistaking the tentative edge. "Hi. You've reached Marcus. I'm sorry I missed your call. Please leave a message and I'll get back to you." Beep.

Silence stretches like an open wound. "Uh. Hi, Marcus. It's Sloane. I'm…" My voice wavers. "I have an envelope for you. Um, your mail, I mean. I'll try you again later. Okay. Bye." I hang up and stare at the screen, half-expecting a callback right away. The moment passes, and all I'm left with is the flood of my own memories.

I'd only met him once. Theo had brought me to the apartment late one night. No explanation, just a quiet "You'll like him" before the door swung open. Marcus had stood in the entryway barefoot, eyes wary—not unfriendly, but like he was weighing me. We stayed maybe an hour and now that I think about it, I haven't been back since. Theo always preferred the privacy of my place.

I grab my coat without really thinking, slipping the envelope into the pocket. If Marcus won't answer my calls, I'll bring this to him. At the very least, it gives me somewhere to be.

The streets feel quiet tonight. A thin layer of frost glitters under the streetlamps, crunching faintly beneath my boots. The shopfronts I pass

11

are mostly dark—an optometrist, a laundromat, a café with chairs stacked on tables. My reflection ghosts in the windows, pale in the dim light, and for a moment I almost don't recognize myself.

I cut across a narrow side street, where the shadows fall deeper. The only sound is the hum of a vending machine outside a shuttered convenience store. Someone's recycling bin has tipped over, its contents rattling in the wind.

When I reach his building, the brick looks darker than I remember, the windows reflecting the night. I push through the heavy outer door.

The stairwell breathes out cold air that smells faintly of dust and stale takeout. Paint curls from the railing, and each step complains beneath my weight. By the time I reach the second floor, my breath is quick—though not from the climb.

At the door, I hesitate. What am I even doing here? But I knock anyway.

Marcus's voice is muffled. "Yeah?"

"It's Sloane." My voice sounds small, uncertain.

There's a pause, then the door unlocks.

Marcus stands there, awkward, eyes flicking away when I look at him. "I wasn't expecting you."

"I know," I say. "Sorry, I just thought I'd bring this by. Save you the trip." I offer up the envelope like a peace offering.

He takes it but doesn't move aside. From the doorway, I catch glimpses: the same couch, same bare walls, same chipped tile in the entryway. But it feels different somehow.

Last time I was here, Theo had dropped his keys on the counter and made some offhand comment about how Marcus was always "weird about shoes." It felt casual. Normal.

Now it feels... staged.

"I could grab Theo's things while I'm here," I say. "If you don't mind. Just to... you know. Get it over with."

Marcus blinks, like I've spoken in another language. "What?"

"His books, clothes..."

He shifts, one hand rubbing the back of his neck, the other still gripping the envelope. "Oh. Right. Yeah, I mean... I think he took most of it with him."

"When he left for the trip?"

"Yeah." His gaze flicks over his shoulder into the apartment, then back to me, like he's checking whether I can see past him.

I let the silence hang.

There's nothing left to say. Not really. But I can't tell if he's hiding something or if grief just looks strange on him.

"Well," I say, backing toward the door. "Thanks. For... letting me bring this by."

Marcus nods, fast. "Yeah. Totally. No problem."

I hesitate at the threshold. "If you find anything of his—"

"I'll let you know."

I offer a tight smile and turn, stepping into the hallway, the door clicking shut behind me.

* * *

The walk back feels longer than the walk there. Maybe because I'm not in a hurry anymore. Or maybe because I'm dragging something invisible behind me.

I don't know this part of the city well. It's mostly quiet residential streets, the trees nearly bare now, their last brittle leaves skittering along the sidewalks in the wind. A thin gray light makes everything feel colder than it should be. I step over a cracked bit of pavement and try to shake off the strange chill that's settled in my chest.

I think he took most of it with him.

That line keeps rattling around in my head. I didn't question it in the moment—maybe because I didn't want to. But now it clangs louder with every step.

Theo didn't have anyone. No parents. No siblings. No storage unit somewhere full of backup furniture. He wasn't sentimental. But he had *things*. A backpack worn soft at the seams. A favorite hoodie he practically lived in. A cracked mug with some pretentious literary quote he claimed was ironic. None of that was in the apartment. Not on the counters. Not in the entryway. Not even in the energy of the place.

And Marcus. God. He'd been trying so hard not to act weird that it just made him weirder. His hands jammed into his pockets like he didn't know what else to do with them.

I think he took most of it with him.

Right. Because when you head out on a weekend hike, you bring your shampoo *and* all traces of your life with you.

I cross the street and pause at the curb, letting a car pass. There's a tightness in my chest I didn't notice before, like my body's only just catching up to what my mind's been circling.

Theo and Marcus were roommates, split the rent, shared the place. That's what I understood. But now that I think back, something feels off about my own memories. I remember Marcus's dishes, his movies, his mess, but I can't remember Theo's toothbrush in the bathroom. Why would their apartment have his books but not his toiletries? And the more I think about it, the more it bugs me.

Theo's parents died when he was eighteen. He didn't have siblings. There wouldn't have been anyone to come and pack up his stuff. So where did it all go?

I grab my laptop and start a search, forcing each keystroke into the frenzied calm of logic and facts. I type in the name of the apartment complex and add the address. Find the contact number. I know the paranoia is getting to me, but it's the only thing that feels like a friend right now.

I stare at the search results, take a deep breath, and dial the first phone number I see. This time, I brace myself for what I might hear.

"Yeah?" The voice is rough, a little irritated.

"Hello?" I stammer. "I'm trying to reach the landlord for Riverside Apartments?"

"Speaking." He sounds even more annoyed. "What is this?"

"I'm—" I falter, surprised by the bluntness of his tone. "I'm calling about Theo."

"Theo?" His voice cuts in with disbelief. "The hell you talking 'bout? You sure you have the right number?"

The question hangs in the air like a trap, and I'm careful not to get caught in it. "Yes. I'm the attorney representing his estate. He recently passed away." I lie.

"Listen, lady. I'm pretty busy here."

I keep my voice steady. "I just need to verify some details to make sure we're talking about the same tenant."

There's a long pause on the line. "Don't have a tenant by that name. Never did."

My heart slams against my ribcage. "Are you sure? I have the address here."

"What address?"

I don't know how much more I can pretend without losing it. "Look, I just need to know if you need any documentation on your end to break the lease."

The landlord lets out an impatient huff. "What did I just tell you? I don't have anyone by that name."

"But—"

"You got the wrong number."

His tone is sharp, final. Then with a click, the call drops.

Chapter 4

Why would he lie about where he lives?

The timeline on the wall stares back at me, each hastily scrawled sticky note an accusation. It's messy grid lines my studio apartment like a conspiracy theorist's shrine. My laptop throws out a blue light, the digital records a pale imitation of what I know happened. Nothing adds up. Nothing makes sense.

What else was he hiding?

Rain lashes the window like the frantic tap of fingers on glass, an impatient rhythm that beats in time with my pulse. The maps, the photos, the half-legible notes crowd my small apartment, leaving just enough room for me to doubt my sanity. An overturned mug drips cold coffee onto the floor, an offering to my own obsessive rituals. I don't even know what I'm looking for anymore, but I know it has to be here, somewhere.

Or maybe I'm just going crazy.

Theo's face floats up from my memory, close enough to touch. That serious look he got when he thought I wasn't watching, when his mask slipped just a little. Who was he, really? And what was I to him? My thoughts swirl with the images of our last months together after a year of dating. The way he'd vanish without warning, then show up at my door, grinning like a magician revealing his favorite trick. I didn't care where he went as long as he always came back.

But this time he didn't.

I fight the flood of memories, wrestle them back into the past where they belong. Every moment I waste on nostalgia is a moment I could be using to find him. To help him. Or...to make him pay. I grab a new pen, write until

16

my hand cramps. Write until I can't tell if I'm hunting for clues or exorcising demons.

He might not even be alive. The thought hits me like it always does—sharp and brutal and sudden—and I have to remind myself to breathe through it. My chest tightens with fear and fury. My mind runs in a thousand directions, wild and tangled and desperate, until I force it to slow down and think rationally. If Theo wanted to vanish, he could. But if someone else wanted me to believe he was still alive, they could do that too.

The rain turns to a low, constant drumming, like fingers tapping on my skull. It follows me from the laptop to the timeline, where I stand, hands on my hips, assessing the chaotic evidence of my obsession. I've seen things no one else would notice, traced threads of connection through the most random facts. I trust my instincts. I have to. I have nothing else.

I count the rings on the other end of the line. Three. Four. A tired voice picks up.

"Boulder P.D." a clipped voice answers, words sharp and practiced.

"Yes, hello," I say, the break in my voice betraying me. "I'm calling about a death. I mean, an accident. Hiking accident. A few weeks ago." My words tumble out, a tangled mess. "I need to know if there's a report."

There's a pause. Not long. Just enough for unease to slip in sideways.

"I can check," the officer says. I hear the click of a keyboard, the rustle of paper. I imagine files pulled from drawers, lists scrolled through, each one a barrier between me and the truth. My free hand drums against the desk, keeping time with my pulse. I close my eyes, try to picture what they're seeing.

"Could you spell that last name for me?" the voice asks, finally.

My heart sinks. "H-A-R-R-I-S."

"Got it." Another pause. Longer this time, the seconds ticking by like taunts. He mutters the name to himself under his breath as he types it, the way someone does when they're double-checking. I hear more clicking, then silence—just the low hum of a fluorescent light overhead and the scrape of his mouse against a desk.

"I'm sorry, ma'am. I don't have anything here under that name."

"What do you mean?" I ask. My voice sounds far away. "It s-should have been reported in mid-January."

"Okay. Let me just…can I put you on hold for a second?"

"Sure." I barely finish the word before the line shifts.

Muzak spills through like a slap. Cheerful saxophone on a death call. Like the universe is mocking me on purpose.

Fifteen seconds. Twenty.

I count again, because it's something to do. Because part of me is still waiting for someone to say they made a mistake—that it's all been processed and yes, yes, of course, we have a file right here.

"Okay…" he says. "I'm looking at reports from January. There's a John Doe found around the 17th—Flatirons area. But, uh… there's no name attached. No ID on the body, and no positive match since. That's all I've got here."

"No," I say quickly. "No, that's not right."

"Ma'am—"

"I was told it was him." The words are too fast, too messy. "Someone called me. From your department. They said it was Theo. They said he was dead. I got a call."

He hesitates, and I can hear something shift. Less defensive now. More careful.

"I understand," he says, and somehow I believe that he might. "But… no one from our department would've reached out. Not without ID confirmation. That would go through the coroner's office—and even then, only after a positive match."

"I'm telling you." My hands are gripping the desk now, white-knuckled. "They came to my apartment. In New York. In uniform. They gave me Theo's watch."

I'm on my feet. Heart pounding, skin too tight. Like if I don't move, I'll explode.

"Ma'am…" he says, gentler now. Like he hears it—that thin edge I'm standing on. "I'm trying to help you. But that kind of in-person notification, especially out-of-state, would've required coordination. Documents. Chain of custody. Signatures. We have none of that."

I don't hear most of what he says after that. Just white noise and the distant roar of something breaking inside me.

"So what are you saying?" I whisper. "That I imagined it?"

"No," he says quickly. "I'm not saying that. I just—" A sigh. The kind people give when they know they're about to be the villain in someone else's story. "Hold on. Please don't hang up."

Click.

Silence.

No music this time. Just my breath in my throat and the sound of the radiator hissing like it's trying to warn me.

A new voice comes on the line.

"This is Lieutenant Greyson. I understand you're calling about a missing person case?"

There's a weariness to him. The voice of someone who's seen too much. Who's already made a dozen calls like this today.

I swallow. My voice is small. "Not missing. I was told he was dead. Theo Harris. Mid-thirties. Dark hair, blue eyes. He went missing in January while hiking near the Flatirons."

He doesn't respond right away. I can hear him pulling up the same system. Typing. Breathing.

"I'm seeing the same file," he says after a moment. "Unidentified male recovered from the base of the Flatirons. No ID. No missing person matches confirmed. Still listed as John Doe."

"No," I whisper. "No, you're not listening. Someone already told me it was him. I got the call. He was dead. I grieved him. I buried him. He's gone. And now you're telling me... what? That none of it was real?"

"Ma'am," Greyson says gently, and that gentleness makes it worse. "I'm not saying it wasn't real. I'm saying no one from Boulder PD made that call."

I stare at the watch on my desk. The watch I was given. Cold, scratched, familiar.

"But...h-he had a badge." It takes effort to keep my voice steady. "The, um. He was in uniform. Came to my door, said his name was, um..." My words are sliding out sideways now, pieces that don't quite fit together. I close my eyes, the memory of his name evading me. "Dunning, I think. Yeah, Officer Dunning."

I'm met with a long, painful silence. If I couldn't still make out the sounds of the precinct in the background, I'd have assumed the call disconnected. Finally, he exhales, low and slow. The kind that never precedes good news.

"Miss...we don't have an Officer Dunning on staff."

"No, that's not—" I pace in a tight circle, hand pressed hard against my chest. "No, he came to my door. My door. In New York. He had the—he had the badge, he said he was with Boulder PD. He said..." I trail off.

I stare at the window. The rain's still going, smearing the city into streaks. Everything in me folds in. I sit like I've forgotten how to stand.

"Then who did I let into my home?"

He doesn't answer.

"W-what do I..." I don't even know what to ask, so I let the sobs come.

Greyson inhales, slow and deliberate. "You should call your local precinct," he says. "Report the impersonation. That's a serious offense. Did he say anything else? Give you anything besides the watch?"

I wipe at my face with the sleeve of my sweatshirt, even though I'm still holding the phone.

"He—he gave me an article," I say. My voice is shaking again, and I hate it. "A newspaper clipping. It was folded up. From... some Colorado paper, I think—" I close my eyes, try to rewind. "He told me they were sure it was Theo. Said the article went out before they confirmed it was him. That it took time because the, uh—" My throat tightens. "Because the body was too damaged. They could only ID him from the watch."

I reach for the drawer in the desk, fumbling with the handle like it's resisting me. The article's there, tearstained and creased from how many times I've unfolded and refolded it. I flatten it against the wood with shaking fingers.

"Do you still have the article?" he asks.

"Yes," I whisper. "And the watch. I kept them both."

"Good," he says. "Don't let them out of your sight. If you can, scan them. Email them to your local precinct, and ask for the detective on call. They'll start a report."

I nod, forgetting he can't see me. I stare at the watch and article on the desk. They're the only thing anchoring me to the idea that I didn't hallucinate the entire thing.

"Let your precinct know I'll be reaching out. Officer Dunning may not exist—but someone went to a lot of trouble to make you believe he did."

My blood goes cold.

Because that's not just impersonation.

That's intent.

* * *

I don't remember hanging up. I don't remember the phone slipping from my fingers, tumbling to the floor. I only know that I'm staring at my notes on the wall, at the empty spaces where truth should be.

Questions stalk me as I pace the room, as I tear through the evidence with frantic hands. Who called? Who knew? I grab a black marker, scrawl my thoughts in bold, angry lines, pin them to the wall. New connections spark and fizzle like faulty wiring.

The rain rattles the windows like a taunt. I close my eyes, feel the weight of exhaustion pressing down.

What if someone else wanted me to believe he was gone?

"Sloane," I hear his voice, a ghost of memory. "Trust me."

I can't. Not anymore.

The pen trembles in my grip as I write out the possibilities, as I add more tangled threads to the web.

The text message was a breadcrumb. A trap?

The rain outside has stopped, leaving an empty quiet, a stillness that lets the noise inside my head take over. I don't want to hear it, don't want to listen to the ugly, frantic voice that says this is hopeless, says I'm chasing a ghost I'll never catch. But it won't stop. I need answers. I need them more than I need air.

On my laptop, the cursor blinks like an accusation. I type, delete, type again. Desperate queries. Search strings. Community watch groups, Reddit threads, hashtags on social media. Theo might be dead, but nothing is certain except the aching void where he used to be. The gaps in the narrative yawn wider, and I tumble through them, clutching at every possibility like a lifeline.

I'm afraid of what it means, of what it says about me that I can't stop, that I'm unraveling, that my world has narrowed to a single, spiraling obsession. But I keep scrolling, keep digging through the quicksand of unanswered questions.

I'm losing my goddamn mind.

The phone sits silent and accusing, a reminder of how far away the truth feels. Of how far away Theo feels. But even as I slump back, exhausted and furious, I know this is the closest I've come to him in weeks.

Maybe I'm looking at it wrong. Maybe there's something else to see. My fingers move over the keys, compelled by need, by longing, by the one thing I can still hold onto.

Hope.

As the laptop's glow dims in the fading light, I wonder how much of myself I'll have left when this is over.

It's all for you, he used to say, but I never knew what he meant. Maybe I never knew anything about him. Maybe I'm a fool to think I know anything now.

What if he's alive? What if he isn't? The questions tighten like a noose, pulling me down into that awful space where I doubt everything. Even myself. This is what obsession does. Who else would want to drive me this crazy? ...Who else could?

The memories come in flashes, relentless and bright, blinding me with their insistence. Theo grinning, confident and sure. I should have known—he was too good at everything.

Too good to be true.

Every smile, every kiss, every soft spoken lie is an electric shock, lighting up the tangled circuitry of my mind. Overloading it. Shutting it down. I'm searching for a hidden message, some trace of the truth left behind in the rubble of us. But it's like digging through the ruins after a bomb has gone off, and all I'm left with are ashes.

It's almost funny. I laugh until it turns to something else, something sharp and edged with panic. Something that sounds more like a sob.

Who was he?

My head's a jumbled mess of too many voices, and I want it to shut up, want them all to leave me alone for just a minute. I need a minute. Just one. But they don't listen, and I'm drowning in questions and ghosts and fragments of a reality I'm not even sure is mine anymore.

Maybe I never really knew him.

My fingers are shaking, fumbling over the keyboard as I pound out a list of names. One of them has to lead me to him, to the truth, to some kind of closure. I can't go on like this. I have to know.

Even if knowing is what destroys me.

Theories swarm my mind like a cloud of gnats, buzzing and biting, leaving me itchy with doubt. What if this is some elaborate hoax? What if I'm the punchline to a joke I can't hear? Panic rises in my throat like bile.

The phone sits there, silent and smug, like it knows more than I do.

I open the text thread. My thumbs hover for a second. Then I type:

Who is this?

Send. Then I add:

What do you want?

Then three dots appear. Typing. Stalling. Vanish. Typing again. Finally, the phone vibrates. My pulse rockets. Theo's number glows on the screen, taunting me. Below it, a location pin and two words.

Come alone.

This time, I laugh, a harsh bark that sounds nothing like me. The sound of a woman on the edge. I clutch the phone, the map, the possibility. It calls out to me like a siren. Upstate New York.

It feels like a lead weight in my hands, this message. Is it a confession? A warning? A cruel trick? The more I look at it, the less I understand, until all that's left is a growing sense of dread and an aching want.

I could delete it. Pretend I never saw it. Block the number. But I don't, because my need to know the truth burns hotter than the fear of what I'll find.

I feel the world tilt, feel myself slipping. Every rational part of me screams not to trust it, not to fall for this. But I'm already gone. Already packing.

I throw clothes into a backpack, hands moving with frantic speed, with a mind of their own. I'm out the door before I can think it through, before I can talk myself out of this. I grab my coat, the keys, the small shred of sanity I have left, and head for the door.

5 A.M. The city is still half asleep, shrouded in fog, the sky a bruised shade of gray. The streets blur by as I drive, a smear of headlights and rain-slicked pavement. I haven't slept in days, but adrenaline and desperation keep me awake, keep me sharp. Keep me going.

Is it him? I can't let myself believe it. Not yet. Not until I see him with my own eyes. I picture his face, the way he'd look at me like I was the only thing in focus. The thought makes me dizzy with longing, with anger, with fear.

If it's a trap, I don't care. I need to know. I need to see.

The miles stretch out ahead of me, endless and uncertain. Just like this search. Just like my life without him. Theo is alive. Theo is dead. And I don't know which possibility terrifies me more.

Chapter 5

This has to be it. I ease the car to a stop, gravel crunching beneath the tires, and glance down at my phone out of habit more than hope. No signal—same as the last dozen times I've checked. Tap the screen. Wait. Nothing. Just an empty map and the indifferent silence of a place that wants to be forgotten. I'm surrounded by trees thick enough to block the sky, the dirt road behind me already disappearing into the forest like it was never there.

I kill the engine. Dust billows past the rearview mirror, then settles. The world goes still.

Ahead, a narrow driveway—choked with weeds and half claimed by nature—leads to a cabin. I thought it would be more... ruined? More in line with the lifeless town I passed through, all peeling paint and boarded windows. A ghost of a place. But this? It's not new, not exactly, but preserved in a way that feels deliberate. Unsettling.

I sit there, staring through the windshield like the cabin might change if I stare long enough. A part of me wants to turn back, retrace the empty miles and vanish before this place notices I'm here. But it's too late for that. I'm already in.

Get out of the car, Sloane.

But I don't move.

The clock says noon, but time doesn't feel real anymore. The air outside is heavy, almost wet, like breathing through gauze. The kind of air that warns you something's coming. I sit with my hands on the wheel, heart ticking in slow, nervous stutters, and try—again—to picture Theo.

I try to see his face. Try to imagine what he'll say, if it's really him. Not just a stranger behind a screen, not just a name borrowed by whoever's been sending those messages. A part of me believes he'll be surprised. Maybe even glad. But hope is a dangerous thing. It has teeth. And right now, it feels a lot like panic.

What am I doing?

A sane person grieves. Or calls their best friend instead of driving hours into the middle of nowhere. But Jessa wouldn't understand, and I never could have explained it anyway. The cabin looms, still and patient, like it's been waiting just as long as I have.

I open the car door and step out. The sound of it closing behind me is sharp, final. Each step toward the porch feels enormous, like I'm crossing into some thin space between memory and reality. The closer I get, the more the fear tightens—pressing into my ribs.

Did he see me pull up? Is he watching?

Don't be paranoid.

But I can't help it. The fear lives in every crack of this place. And still, under the fear, there's something else: a terrible, electric want. A need that burns so hot it hurts.

I have to know.

I climb the steps. The porch groans under my weight. The front door hangs slightly ajar, like it's been left open for me. A trap. A welcome. Maybe both.

"Theo?" I whisper.

It comes out broken, the edges ragged. Not even a word—more like a breath torn in half. It echoes inside the doorway and dies there, unanswered.

I stand frozen at the threshold. One foot in, one foot out, like crossing over might change something, might make this real. I almost turn back and drive until the forest spits me out and the road makes sense again. But then I step forward.

And the cabin holds its breath.

The silence crowds in, and it feels like my lungs are going to burst. The seconds stretch, too tightly.

"Theo?"

My voice doesn't sound like my own. It bounces off the walls and fades. Just like he did. I'm met with silence. There's no reply, no footsteps, no warmth of another presence. I'm alone.

The door yawns open behind me, a route of escape. I glance back, just once, and the afternoon light seems dimmer, more unfriendly than before. As if the outside has given up on me, too.

I tell myself I'll only stay a little while, that if I don't find what I'm looking for, I'll leave. I'll drive far and fast, and this time I won't look back.

The light in the living room glows warm, but not welcoming. It feels off, like a set someone built from memory, every detail a little too precise. A throw blanket draped just so over the couch. A mug beside a book I don't recognize, its spine too stiff to have ever been read.

I touch the edge of the mug. Cold.

I keep moving.

A chessboard waits on the coffee table, mid-game. One side winning. I don't know enough to tell which. Theo never played chess. At least, I don't think he did.

I try to remember—did we ever talk about that? Would I know if he had? A chill laces through my spine.

The kitchen is spotless. No crumbs, no spills, no signs of life—except the coffee pot, still faintly warm.

Someone's here. Or they were.

I open the fridge. Milk. Strawberries. A bottle of wine I haven't seen in years.

I stare at it for a long time. Theo brought that wine to my birthday once. We drank it on the floor of his apartment and laughed until two in the morning.

He wouldn't remember the label. Right?

The thought drops hard, splitting the moment in half.

What if this wasn't a message from Theo at all? What if someone found his phone? His name? What if this was never about him...but about me?

I lean against the counter, dizzy.

Drawers. Cabinets. I open them one by one, not sure what I'm looking for. A clue. A note. A mistake.

The second drawer on the left sticks before giving way.

Inside: a single Polaroid.

It's me.

I'm at the gas pump, fingers wrapped tight around the nozzle, the cold metal digging into my palm as fuel seeps steadily into the tank. The morning light is pale and brittle, the air sharp enough to sting my lungs.

I never heard the shutter. Never sensed the eyes on me.

Now, my stomach twists, bile threatening to rise. Because this photo was taken hours ago. On my way here.

I turn in a slow circle, my eyes scanning every shadow, every doorway, like something might shift. Step forward. Speak. But the cabin stays still.

My breath feels wrong in my chest, too fast and too shallow, like I'm forgetting how to do it right.

Who took this?

I move. Back into the hallway, I pass the bathroom. Spotless. A single toothbrush. A bottle of cologne I recognize instantly.

I don't stop. I don't want to breathe it in.

There's a door at the end of the hall. Closed.

I pause.

The silence tightens. My fingers brush the handle. The door creaks open.

At first, I don't understand what I'm seeing.

A dim room. A single bulb hanging from the ceiling, its glow sickly and yellow. And the walls—God. They're covered.

Photographs. Hundreds, tacked up with pushpins, layered over each other like scales. Screenshots from my social media accounts. Camera phone images, some taken from a distance, some from terrifyingly close.

Me.

All of them—me. Laughing. Walking. Sleeping. At the grocery store. At the park. In my living room. In my bed. My knees buckle, and I grab the doorframe to stay upright. Everywhere I turn, there I am. My life, my face, my body, dissected and displayed in a silent kind of violence. Frozen in time. Out of context. Out of reach. And there's something worse in knowing some of these moments happened before I met him. Before I ever knew his name.

How long? How long had he been watching me?

One photo is circled. My birthday, two years ago. I'm blowing out candles, surrounded by friends. I remember that night—I remember thinking it was perfect. My breath shortens, becomes jagged.

I spot another: me leaving my therapist's office. Another: me crying on my front steps. Another: me in the window of my apartment, brushing my hair.

I was the story. The game. The prize.

There's a photo of me from yesterday. Standing in my kitchen, holding my phone, looking confused. Looking scared.

The exact moment I got the last text from him or…whoever it was.

I want to scream, want to shut my eyes, want to run until I forget this place. But I do none of those things. I stand there, frozen, caught in the chaos, caught in this web.

Caught.

The wall stretches on and on. Screenshots of texts I sent, typed out and printed like they're part of a case file. Notes in handwriting that isn't mine. Observations. Theories. Dates.

It's all for you.

I stagger backward, breath sawing in and out of me. The light flickers once, then steadies. The bulb hums like it's breathing. Like it's alive. I can't look away. I want to. I want to rip the pictures down, tear the whole room apart, but my body betrays me.

This is why he led me here. Not for answers. For this. To see myself the way he sees me. To see how little of me was ever truly mine.

Everything I want is right here.

My vision tunnels. Panic floods in, fast and hot, tightening around my ribs. I stumble back through the doorway, knocking into a chair, catching myself on the wall, half-falling into the hallway. I press my palms to my ears, willing his words from my head, but it doesn't work.

I love you more than you know.

The air feels thinner out here, but not better. Not safer. I don't know how I get to the front door. I don't remember crossing the room. I only know the moment the afternoon air hits my face like a slap.

I'm outside. My feet sink into the dirt. The trees close in around me. The world feels both wide open and impossibly small. The cabin looms behind me like a mouth ready to close. My heart is a hammer in my chest, loud and endless. My breath comes in ragged bursts.

I don't know where to go. I don't know what's real.

A cold certainty presses against the back of my skull. This…this is how he knows me so well. Not because he loved me. Not because he cared. I hate him. I hate myself for not hating him enough.

Chapter 6

"Sloane."

I'd laugh if it didn't mean unraveling. Instead, I turn.

Theo stands at the edge of the trees, hands tucked into the pockets of his jacket like he just wandered out for air. The same easy smile. The same eyes I used to dream about. It's like no time has passed. Like he didn't vanish. Like he didn't fake his own death.

My breath catches hard in my throat. My whole body is suddenly, stupidly aware of itself—of him.

He walks toward me, boots crunching over dead grass. "You found me," he says, like it's a pleasant surprise. Like this is some kind of game. There's pride in his voice. Warmth. Like I'm supposed to be glad.

I freeze. If I move, I might fall into him. I might forget. I might forgive. And I can't forget what I saw inside that cabin.

His footsteps slow as he nears, his hand brushing my arm with maddening tenderness—like we just ran into each other at the grocery store, like I haven't spent weeks drowning in grief and confusion.

"Sloane," he murmurs again, as if that word alone can stitch me back together.

My brain tries to catch up with my body. "Theo."

He smiles, slow and soft. "God, I missed you."

I take a single step back. Not a full retreat. Just enough to breathe. Enough to keep distance without alerting him that I'm afraid. Because I *can't* be afraid. Not visibly.

He doesn't react. Either he doesn't notice... or he's pretending not to.

Which is worse?

"I thought you were dead," I say, the words dry and brittle. "There was a body."

"There had to be," he says, as if it's obvious.

My stomach twists. "There was a newspaper article. Someone came to my house and told me it was you."

"I'm sorry." His voice lowers. "Someone was after me. Someone dangerous."

That's a lie. The cabin wasn't the lair of a hunted man. It was a shrine.

"And the man in the article…?"

"An…unfortunate bystander," he says.

The way he says it makes my skin crawl. I wonder if the man was already dead and Theo saw an opening. Or is it worse than that?

What is he capable of?

I've been quiet a moment too long, and he scrambles to explain. "It was the only way to keep you safe." Forced sincerity, almost saccharine, drips from his voice. "If they knew I was alive, they'd have come after you, too."

Safe. The word sounds rotten. *Safe from who, Theo? From you?*

I hold his gaze a fraction too long.

Don't flinch. Don't show him you know.

"Then why bring me here?"

There. A pause. Barely a beat—but I catch it. His smile tightens. Something flickers behind his eyes.

"Because things changed," he says, voice smooth, practiced. "I needed to see you. I needed you to know."

Know what? That he's been watching me sleep? That he knows where I buy my coffee, who I call when I'm scared?

"Know what?" I ask.

"That I'm alive. That I'm okay." The words hit somewhere between longing and manipulation. They're familiar, perfectly shaped. Theo's always been good with words.

I blink once, slow and careful. If I let myself feel anything, I might run. And I can't run. Not yet. I nod. I tell myself to breathe. To survive the next five minutes. Then maybe the next.

"I…I wasn't sure it was you," I say instead. "The texts. The coordinates. I thought—" I stop myself before I say I thought someone was messing with me. Hunting me. The photos swim in my mind.

"I'm sorry. I really am. It wasn't supposed to happen like this."

Then why did it?

I press my arms tight across my chest, holding myself together in the absence of logic. In the presence of him.

Theo glances toward the horizon. The sun is dipping low, bleeding gold across the sky. Shadows creep across the field like fingers. Goosebumps prick my arms.

"You must be cold," he says.

I hesitate. Not because I'm cold. Because I don't know who he is anymore. And I hate that some part of me—some stupid, trembling part—still loves him anyway.

But I nod.

And I follow him inside.

* * *

The cabin swallows me as soon as I step through the threshold.

Warm air meets my skin, thick with the scent of smoke and cedar and something sweet underneath it—like pine or cologne lingering in the walls. The door clicks shut behind me with a sound that feels like a lock turning.

Theo moves ahead of me, casual, quiet, as though this is just any night. As though I haven't spent weeks grieving him, unraveling.

He doesn't offer me a seat. Doesn't ask if I'm okay. He just stands in front of the fire, silhouetted by its flickering light like he's been waiting for me there forever.

He turns to face me, and his expression shifts—melting into something tender. Something dangerous.

"You don't have to be scared," he says, stepping closer.

I want to laugh, but my throat won't cooperate.

"I'm not scared," I lie.

He smiles like he knows I am. "Good." His hand reaches out again, brushing my cheek this time. "You're perfectly safe." I realize he's referring to his lie and I wonder if there's any chance of it being real. At this point, I doubt my own name.

His touch is familiar—muscle memory, heart memory—but something under it feels... off. There's a weight behind the gentleness, something that hums just beneath the surface. A tension. A threat, disguised as affection.

I flinch inside but don't let it show. I need to think. I need to get my bearings. I need him to believe I'm still his.

"Everything is just happening so fast," I murmur.

He takes my hands in his, thumbs brushing over my knuckles like he used to do when I was anxious. "Ask me anything."

The invitation is too smooth. I test it, meeting his gaze. "What changed?"

"I missed you. That's all."

That's not all.

"But if you were in danger," I press, "if someone was after you, why now? Why lead me here just to say you're alive?"

There's a beat of silence. Then, softly, "Because I'm not in danger anymore."

That's new. That's not what he said before. I nod, even as my chest tightens.

He watches my face as though he's studying the way truth lands. Or the way lies take root.

I've made my choice now. Not to trust. To survive. I let my body soften. Lower my defenses, or at least make it look like I have. My posture eases.

"I didn't know if you'd come if I told you everything."

"Maybe I wouldn't have," I admit. Not accusing. Just honest enough.

He moves closer, and I resist the urge to step back. I let his hands slide to my waist. Familiar pressure. Anchoring. Or maybe controlling. It's hard to tell now.

His gaze dips to my mouth. He leans forward, and I let him kiss me. It's all I've wanted for weeks. It's gentle. Familiar. But under the softness, there's something else. A hunger I don't remember.

My body remembers this. How to respond. How to give him what he wants.

I make my breath catch—just once, soft. I close my eyes when his lips find mine, let the illusion bloom. It's easier when I don't think too much. Easier if I pretend I'm someone who still believes him.

His hands undress me slowly, reverently, like he's unwrapping something fragile. But I'm not fragile anymore. I'm watching everything.

The window is small, maybe just big enough to crawl through, though I'd need something to break the latch. The desk chair looks solid. The lamp on the nightstand is heavy, ceramic. There's a set of keys hanging on a hook by the door. I memorize the sound they made when we walked in—a faint metallic jingle.

Every touch, every kiss, I respond to like muscle memory. I breathe when I'm supposed to. Whisper his name when he wants me to. I keep my movements fluid, willing. But my eyes never stop moving.

There's a water glass on the floor near the bed, half-full. I count three steps to the door, four to the dresser. I wonder if the rug beneath the bed hides anything. A trap door. A weapon. A second shrine.

I feel the shift in him, the moment tenderness turns into possession. He pulls me tighter, his breath uneven. I match his rhythm, meet his movements, and keep my thoughts buried deep behind my eyes. His weight is both comforting and suffocating. His touch, practiced and persuasive. I feel him trying to erase my fear with desire.

But it doesn't work. God, it doesn't work.

I feel everything. My skin knows this is not safety. My nerves are lit up, not from pleasure, but from awareness. The sharp edge of being trapped. Still, I give him what he wants.

Because I need time. Because I don't know what he'll do if I say no.

When it's over, he gathers me against him with the ease of old habits. His arm settles across my waist, fingers splayed.

"I missed this," he whispers. "I missed you."

I lie still, my cheek against the pillow, my body cooling in the aftermath.

His breathing slows. Deepens. He's drifting now, but I don't sleep. I keep my eyes open in the dark, every muscle still, every nerve alert. My thoughts spin, fast and sharp. The shrine. The lies. The trap he lured me into.

I count the seconds between his breaths. I wait for them to even out, for his grip to loosen. Then, inch by inch, I slide from beneath his arm.

His hand twitches but doesn't tighten. I hold my breath as I shift my weight, rolling off the bed with a quiet practiced in grief and fear. My feet hit the floor. I don't stand right away—I crouch, listening. Watching.

Theo doesn't stir.

I reach for my clothes silently, dressing with the precision of someone who's done this before—who's escaped worse. Then I start to move.

The cabin waits in silence, full of secrets and soft footsteps. And I am no longer pretending.

Chapter 7

Light on the balls of my feet, breath shallow, heartbeat loud, I move through the dark like I'm trying not to wake a monster. The air feels too still. Too quiet. My skin itches with the memory of that room—the shrine, the wall, the photos.

Snapshots of my life stolen from the shadows. Of moments I never knew were being watched—eating breakfast by my window, tying my shoes at the park, smiling at a stranger on the subway.

I can't unsee it. I can't unfeel the sickness twisting in my gut.

My body hums with adrenaline, and I know what this is now—this isn't heartbreak. It isn't a coincidence. I've been hunted. Tracked. Profiled like a lab rat. And not just recently. For months. Maybe years.

I need to get out. Now.

I whip around the living room, eyes scanning every surface for a landline. A charger. A signal bar blinking from somewhere.

Nothing.

I pat down my jeans and hoodie, my movements frantic. No phone.

Where—? My heart stutters. *Where was the last place I had it?*

Memory stabs through the panic. My jacket pocket. I had it there when I walked into the cabin. I remember checking my texts. Sliding it back in.

My jacket is still hanging by the door. I tear through both pockets. Empty.

He took it.

Fuck!

The fireplace behind me crackles too loudly. Or maybe it's just the silence wrapping around it that's so deafening. The shadows flicker like they're watching.

I need to move.

I scan the space again—living room, kitchen, one hallway leading deeper into the cabin. I already know there are no neighbors nearby, nothing for miles. I have no way to call for help. But maybe—maybe there's something else. A map. A car key. Anything.

I move methodically, even as panic rides me like a shadow. Drawer by drawer in the kitchen. Cabinets. Under the sink. A junk drawer full of old batteries and rubber bands. Nothing helpful. Nothing sharp. Not even a knife. The block on the counter is empty.

Why are the—

A sharp crack cuts through my thoughts. A floorboard.

I freeze.

Then slowly crouch near the edge of the living room. One of the corner planks is crooked. Slightly warped. Not quite aligned with the rest. I run a finger along its edge and feel the uneven lift. A hiding place.

Heart hammering, I wedge my fingernail beneath the plank. It resists at first, then gives way with a soft creak. I lift it, and a breath catches in my throat.

There's a box beneath it. A metal one, the kind with a latch. I hesitate for only a second before flipping it open.

Photos. At first glance, they look like more of me. My stomach drops. But no—these aren't me. Different women. Young. Smiling. Reading in cafés, walking down streets. But the longer I look, the more I see it—they all look a little like me. Similar jawlines. Similar builds. Hair shades that hover around brunette or auburn. There's something almost systematic about it, like he has a type.

Nestled between the photos are ID cards. Driver's licenses. Each one with a different name. But the faces—they could be cousins. Sisters.

I lift one and study it. Amanda Leigh. 28. Oregon. Then another. Sierra Holt. 30. North Carolina. And another. Evelyn Barnes.

I know that name. Why do I know that name?

Beneath the IDs, there's jewelry. A ring. A delicate necklace with a cracked pearl. Little pieces. Personal things. Souvenirs.

I gag.

It's the wall all over again, but worse. I'm not the first. I may not be the last.

No. Not if I can help it.

I fumble backward, nearly knocking the whole box from my lap. I'm breathing too fast. My fingers won't stop shaking. My chest is tight.

What did he do to them? What is he planning to do to me?

I shove everything back into the box, force myself to nestle it exactly the way I found it. Close the lid. Fit it back into the floor. Lower the board. Cover the evidence.

I don't know why I do it—instinct, maybe. Or some desperate part of me clinging to the hope that if he doesn't know I know, I'll have time to run.

I stand, swaying. I have to leave. Now.

I lurch for the front door and wrap my fingers around the handle. I twist. It doesn't move.

I tug harder. It rattles in place. I stumble back, then dart for the side door. Bathroom window—too small. Kitchen—nothing. I race through the hallway and try the back. Locked. No keyhole. Just a flat, unbroken knob and another bolt above it.

I whirl around—Theo is standing there.

Blocking the hallway.

He's still. Calm. A mug in one hand. His other hand rests at his side, casual—almost amused.

"Looking for something?" he asks, voice light. Friendly.

My mouth opens, but nothing comes out. I force a breath. Try to smile. "I—I just wanted some water."

He watches me for a moment, his expression unreadable. Then his mouth curves.

"You were never good at pretending," he whispers. "Not really."

Something in his voice shifts. Lowers. Darkens. A chill races down my spine. My whole body goes cold.

That's when I know—he wanted me to find the box. The wall. All of it.

This wasn't a mistake. It's part of the game. The realization slams into me like a truck. I blink—and he steps forward.

I bolt.

I throw myself past him, elbowing hard into his side. The mug crashes to the ground. I hear him grunt behind me, but I don't look back.

I shove a chair into the hallway behind me, slam the coat rack down, send a lamp crashing as I sprint through the main room.

Every door is locked. Every window sealed.

I claw at the living room window, yanking, rattling, hitting it with the heel of my palm. It doesn't budge.

Behind me, his voice is still calm. Still infuriatingly in control.

"I studied you, Sloane," he says. "For months."

I whirl around. He's moving slowly, stepping over debris. Not running. Just... watching.

"Your routines. Your habits. Your tells," he continues. "You think you were hard to read. You weren't."

I back toward the hallway. My feet crunch on broken glass.

"The day we met?" he says. "At the coffee shop?" A smile tugs at the corner of his mouth. "You really believed that was random?"

He's enjoying this.

I feel like I'm watching a stranger wear Theo's skin.

I shake my head. "Why?"

He cocks his head. "Because you were perfect."

Memories crash into me. The way he always knew exactly what I needed. How he always "just happened" to be nearby. I force myself to breathe. Steady. Controlled. Because now I understand something else—he needs to believe I'm weak.

I drop my shoulders, widen my eyes. "Please," I whisper, voice trembling. "I—I didn't mean to go through your things." I let tears spill, let the panic show.

My fingers inch behind me, searching blindly. Smooth wood. Something soft. Then, cold and solid. Heavy. Ceramic. I curl my hand around it, feeling the weight like permission.

The lamp arcs through the air in one swift, silent motion before it shatters against his temple with a sickening crack. His grunt is low, feral, surprised. He stumbles, hand reaching for the side of his head as shards rain around us. Blood blooms beneath his hairline like a crimson flower.

I don't wait to see if he falls.

Floorboards shriek beneath my steps, the air clawing at my lungs as I hurl myself into the hallway. The front door is still locked—I know that now—but I slam into it anyway, shoulder-first, out of reflex or hope or blind terror. It doesn't budge. Behind me, the sound of broken ceramic and Theo's low grunt echoes through the room like a memory I'll never stop hearing.

* * *

There's an attic. I know there is—I saw the pull cord earlier in the hallway, right outside the surveillance room. I sprint for it, heart hammering in my throat, praying the cord hasn't been moved.

It's there. Hanging. I jump for it, grip it, yank with all my weight. The stairs creak down like a scream.

I scramble up them without looking, every step groaning beneath me. The attic smells like dust and mothballs and something sweet gone rotten. I don't wait to figure out what. I crawl forward into the dark, dragging the ladder up behind me and slamming the trapdoor shut just as I hear his footsteps approach.

Silence.

Then a soft knock from below.

"Sloane."

My whole body goes still.

"You're not thinking straight," he calls. "Just… come down. I'll explain everything."

I press my hand over my mouth.

The trapdoor shifts, testing my weight. I lie flat over it, every muscle braced, waiting for the push. For him to come up anyway. But he doesn't.

The attic is barely lit—just a sliver of moonlight leaking through a dirty window. I search by feel, dragging my hands along the walls, the boxes. I find an old duffel bag, musty and half-zipped, filled with boots and a raincoat. A flare gun, half-buried beneath a blanket.

Yes.

I snatch it, check the barrel. No flares—just the gun. My heart sinks, but I shove it into my waistband and slide over to the window.

It's too narrow for me to fit through. But the wood around it is soft. Rotted. I dig my fingers into the frame, tug at the corners.

It gives. Not all at once, but enough.

If I can find something to pry with—the flare gun. I wedge it under the frame and lever it back. The window groans, cracks. I twist harder. Suddenly, the frame snaps free—and my momentum carries me sideways. My elbow slams into the floor.

I bite back a scream.

Through the window, the trees are darker than the sky, a sea of jagged black. No lights. No roads. Just forest. But it's a way out.

I crawl up onto the wall, brace my hands on the frame, and lower myself through, feet first.

It's a twelve-foot drop.

I breathe once. Then let go.

I hit the ground hard, knees buckling, air knocked from my chest. The cold bites—midnight mountain air, sharp and punishing. I roll to my feet, stagger forward, and run. No flashlight. No path. Branches whip across my face. Roots threaten to snap my ankles. The night is all sound and shadow—the rustle of leaves, the whisper of wind, the pounding of blood in my ears.

I run until my lungs burn. Until my legs scream. Until I can't hear anything but the echo of my own breath.

Then I stop. I duck behind a tree, kneel in the underbrush, and listen. Nothing. No footsteps. No Theo. I think I've lost him.

Until I hear the voice.

I twist, my whole body snapping toward the sound. It's his voice. But it's not coming from nearby. It's coming from… above?

A speaker. Hidden.

"You're clever, Sloane. That's what I love about you. You adapt. You survive.

42

That's why I picked you."

My blood goes ice cold. He wired the woods.

There's a hiss of static, then: "You've always been good at puzzles. How about a game?"

"No," I whisper. "No, no, no."

The speaker cuts off. Then another voice—soft, female—comes from a different direction.

Me. It's my voice. A recording.

Yes, I'm the attorney representing his estate...

Sorry, I just thought I'd bring this by. Save you the trip.

I'm fine.

The forest echoes with fragments of me, disembodied and uncanny. They twist around the trees like ghosts.

Theo's shrine wasn't just walls. This whole place is his masterpiece.

I break into a sprint again—no direction, just away. The terrain dips. The slope sharpens. I don't see the edge until it's too late.

I tumble—hard.

Brush and rock tear at my arms. My shoulder slams into something solid. I flip once, twice, land hard. Pain blooms behind my eyes.

Everything goes quiet.

When I wake, it's darker.

How is it darker?

I'm lying on a slope, half-hidden by ferns. My leg is bleeding—nothing deep, just messy. My ankle protests when I stand, but it holds. The ground is cold and unforgiving beneath me, roots pressing into my back, ferns curling like fingers around my legs. My ankle throbs where it twisted, and I taste blood where I bit the inside of my cheek during the fall. The night air scrapes in and out of my lungs in ragged bursts. For a second—maybe longer—I don't move.

I just breathe.

The canopy sways above me, whispering in a language I don't understand. But I'm listening now. To everything.

I push myself upright, gasping as pain flares down my leg. My whole body screams in protest, but I don't stop. Twigs snap beneath my feet as I limp forward, every step cutting through fog and panic. My foot catches on a root. I stumble, swear, keep going.

Somewhere behind me, the cabin sits silent, pretending to sleep.

Chapter 8

Branches whip my face. My bare feet pound frostbitten earth. My lungs are on fire. But there's a rhythm to it, this escape—one-two-breathe, one-two-bleed.

Somewhere behind me, he's watching. Or following. Or just waiting.

I don't know. But I can feel it.

The ground slopes down, and I lurch through the trees, the landscape folding in on itself—same bark, same frozen ground, same silent shadows. My mind reels through the last twelve hours, trying to find a seam in the memory where things *felt* real.

None of it does.

A glint ahead. Moonlight bouncing off glass.

My car.

Relief threatens to undo me. Get to the car. Get out. Call for help. Scream if I have to. I'll drive until I hit pavement. Until I see headlights. Until someone tells me I'm safe and I believe them.

That's the plan.

The only one I've got.

Frost crunches underfoot. And there it is: my car, tucked into the edge of the woods, just as I left it. Close enough to escape if things went bad. Something in my chest shifts. Not fear—something sharper. I approach slowly, eyes scanning the area. No movement. I slow, every muscle trembling. Knees weak. It looks untouched. No broken windows. No footprints. No signs of tampering.

Except the feeling in my gut.

The awful *knowing*.

I reach the door and try the handle. It gives, unlocked.

My fingers twitch—habit. I reach for my keys. *Not there*. I check my other pocket. Empty.

My stomach drops. When? When did he take them?

I slide into the driver's seat and slam the door. Lock it. A thin barrier between me and whatever version of hell I just crawled out of. The quiet inside the car is suffocating, like I sealed myself into a tomb.

The heat's dead without the engine. My toes are already numb. I curl them, trying to coax blood back into them, press my feet to the floor vents like it might make a difference.

I grab the fleece blanket from the backseat, wrap it tight around my shoulders. I shake so hard I can barely think.

Phone.

I reach into my waistband, certain I tucked it there when I left the cabin—but it's gone.

No. No no no.

I dig frantically through the seat cushions. Under the blanket. Nothing.

Either I dropped it during the sprint, or he took it too. That thought makes me want to gag.

I scan the dashboard, looking for something I can use without the keys. I flip open the glove box. Nothing but insurance papers and an expired pack of gum. I rest my head against the steering wheel. This is the part in movies where the heroine screams. Instead, I sit in the silence, breath fogging the glass. Waiting. Wishing. Dreading.

A red light blinks deep in the woods. A camera? I can't be sure.

"Okay. Okay. Okay." I whisper the words like a mantra.

Then I remember—the tire iron. Trunk.

I open the door again, blanket still wrapped around me, and stumble toward the back of the car. My fingers fumble with the latch.

The trunk pops open. I lean in—reach for the iron—and the ground disappears.

No sound, no warning.

Just a sickening drop.

I fall.

Branches and leaves collapse beneath me, and then I'm slamming into cold, packed dirt five feet below, my shoulder cracking against something hard. Pain explodes across my ribs. My scream gets swallowed by the earth.

* * *

I lie there for a second, stunned. Dizzy.

The air tastes like dirt and iron. I cough and blink up at the sky—just a square of night, framed by broken twigs. I shift, and pain screams through my side. Something hard jabs at my thigh. I fumble blindly and pull it free.

My phone. It lights up in my hand. My blood turns to ice. This isn't just a trap. It's a taunt.

I almost throw the phone, but I stop myself. Instead, I clutch it to my chest like a lifeline. The screen glows against my skin, mocking me.

I breathe. Count to four.

Now what?

The pit is too deep to climb out with just my hands. No roots. No steps. No ladder. Just me, dirt, and the smell of cold rot.

Panic claws at my throat, but I force it down.

Think.

I shift, hissing as sore muscles protest. Bruised, not broken. Dirt clings to my palms, grit grinding into my skin. Above me, the edge is just out of reach.

But not impossible.

I search the floor of the pit—twigs, small stones, a snapped piece of branch thick as my wrist. I drag it to the wall and jam it into the corner like a brace.

It bends, flexes. Not strong enough.

I need something more.

I remember the trunk—the lid is still open. Maybe—

I take off the blanket, tie it in a makeshift loop around my waist, then grip the stick again and wedge it harder into the wall. I jam my bare toes into the dirt, clawing for purchase.

It takes three tries. Maybe four. The first time, I slip and land hard on my elbow. The second time, the stick breaks. On the third, I cry out, a sharp sound I try to swallow. But I don't stop. Because this is what he wants.

He wants me to stay down here. To feel hunted. Trapped. Powerless. He wants me broken. And I won't give him that.

I jam the broken stick into the dirt like a wedge and shove myself upward. My foot catches a groove. My hand snags a root. I climb.

My fingers scrape raw. Dirt fills my nose and mouth. My shoulder howls in protest. But I get one hand on the rim. Then the other. Then I'm out.

I collapse on the frozen ground, cheek pressed to gravel and frost. Gasping. Shaking. Alive. I roll over, blinking up at the stars. Cold burns under my skin like acid. I curl into myself, gripping the phone again. My fingers hover over the home screen. No signal. *Of course.*

He designed every second of this. I sit up slowly, still trembling. My eyes scan the trees. The shadows. Without thinking, I clamber to my feet and rush toward the treeline, cold nipping at my bare heels.

The trees thin for a second—just a moment of space, of light—and I stumble into it, sag against the nearest trunk. I bend over, hands on my knees, the cold bark pressing into my spine. I look back the way I came.

No movement. No footsteps. No Theo. But I feel him. That's the part that turns my stomach. I feel him like a second pulse under my skin. Watching. Waiting. Letting me think I'm escaping. Because that's what this is, isn't it?

A game.

A script.

He let me find the photos. He let me find the box. He wanted me to run.

That's why the floorboard was already loose. That's why the shrine was so precise, so deliberate.

Because this isn't just about surveillance. It's about performance.

He faked his death so I would grieve, unravel, isolate myself from everyone who could protect me. So that when he returned, I would already be hollowed out. And no one would question it if I... disappeared. No one would ask why Sloane couldn't go on anymore.

They'd say: *She never recovered from losing him.*

They'd say: *Grief does strange things.*

They'd say: *She gave up.*

I choke back bile and wipe my mouth with the back of my shaking hand. He's still controlling the narrative. Even in death. Especially in death.

I push off the tree and start walking, slower now. Quiet. Listening. Thinking.

If he's this far ahead, I can't outpace him.

I have to out-think him. I could run. I could keep going, try to reach the next road, the next town. Follow moonlight and guesswork. Freeze to death before sunrise. If I keep running, I'm playing his game. Dancing his steps. Sprinting into every trap he's already laid. Because there are probably more. He mapped out the entire escape. Dug the holes. Removed the knives. Took my phone, my keys, my control.

He knows me. He knows I'd run. So I can't.

I clench my jaw, rage building behind my ribs. I stare toward the dark silhouette of the cabin, looming just beyond the tree line.

If this is his game, I have to stop playing by his rules. I won't give him the satisfaction. If he wants prey, I'll be something else. Something with teeth.

It goes against every instinct I have. Every cell in my body screams *get out*. Get help. Keep going until the trees thin and the world makes sense again. But there's no one out here. No signal. No town nearby. No savior coming.

If I want to survive this, I have to face it. Face *him*. I rise, slow and unsteady, brushing frozen dirt from my arms. My legs tremble, but I make them move. Back toward the cabin.

Not because I'm brave.

Because the only way out of this… is through him.

Chapter 9

I crouch behind the tree line, breath clouding the air, heart knocking against my ribs. I've come full circle—literally. I fled this place in panic, bled on the forest floor, nearly passed out on the side of a hill. And now I'm back. Because running didn't work. Because he took my choices away the second he started watching me. Now it's my turn to watch him.

I scan the perimeter again. The front door's shut tight. Curtains drawn. No lights on inside, but the faint flicker of firelight still glows between the boards. I shift lower, knees biting into the frozen ground.

Then I see it.

A basement window—low to the ground, half-covered by brittle shrubs, left cracked just wide enough to catch moonlight. Open. And that's all I need.

No part of me believes it's an accident. But it's the only point of entry. And if I'm careful, quiet, deliberate—it might be the sole advantage I get.

I move fast but silent, staying low. Brush aside the dead branches, press my fingertips against the window's edge. I wait, listening. No footsteps. No creak of floorboards. I push it open and slide through.

The moment I hit the basement floor, the cold slaps the breath from my lungs.

I stay crouched beneath the open window, limbs shaking, breath locked in my throat. Every inch of me is screaming to bolt back into the woods, but I don't move.

Not yet.

I ease the window shut behind me, slow and careful. The lock clicks gently into place. Too loud. Everything feels too loud down here.

It's darker than I expected. Just outlines—shelves, crates, old furniture stacked like forgotten bones. It's silent, save for the quiet hum of something running in the far corner, maybe a freezer or an old dehumidifier. The rest of the house above me feels unnervingly still.

I scan the basement. Boxes are stacked along the walls. Shelves line the far side.

No knives. No tools. No weapons. Not surprising.

My hands graze across a dusty sheet covering a pile of furniture. I lift the edge and find a stack of old wooden chairs, legs tangled, paint chipped. I grip one and try to pull it free. It doesn't budge at first. I give it another yank.

The chair screeches across the concrete floor. I freeze, stomach dropping. The sound ricochets off the walls like a scream.

Above me, floorboards creak.

Shit. He heard that.

I wrench the chair harder, urgency overtaking fear. The frame splinters as it comes loose. The back cracks against the wall. I flip it over and slam it, once, twice, until one of the legs snaps off in my hands. It's not smooth—it's jagged, uneven. But it's heavy. Pointed. Good enough. Footsteps above me now. Slow. Testing. He knows something's off.

I crouch again, pressing into the shadows behind a stack of crates, the broken chair leg clenched in my fist. My hands are shaking so hard I have to press the splintered end into my thigh just to keep from dropping it.

The stairs groan. I squeeze my eyes shut for half a second. I didn't plan this far. I didn't plan at all. I came back because I couldn't let him win. Because the only thing worse than being hunted was doing nothing. But now he's coming. He's coming and I don't have a plan, just a piece of wood and a prayer.

The door at the top of the stairs creaks open. Light spills down. I grip the chair leg tighter. His shadow appears in the stairwell. The stairs creak once. Then again.

I crouch lower, tightening my grip on the jagged chair leg. My breath catches in my throat and holds. My whole body is one tight wire.

Another creak. He's coming down. I don't breathe. I don't think. I just wait.

A sliver of light spills down the stairwell, and then his shadow stretches across the floor. Another step. His foot hits the concrete. Closer.

I rise—slow, careful, silent—and when I see the blur of his shoulder, the edge of his neck—I swing. The wood connects with a sick, hollow crack. He stumbles, hard, a grunt tearing from his throat. I don't look back.

I race up the stairs, two at a time. My knee nearly gives but I don't stop, don't breathe, don't feel anything except the wild roar of blood in my ears.

Almost there.

Almost—his hand closes around my ankle.

I scream—sharp and ragged—twist, and kick back with everything I have.

My heel catches his face—nose or cheek or mouth, I don't know—but it lands hard. He lets go with a sharp curse, and I lurch forward, slam my shoulder into the basement door, and throw the bolt home.

Click.

I fall against it, gasping. Shaking. Below me, silence. No pounding. No threats. Just the thick, terrifying stillness of a man regrouping. I scramble to my feet and back away from the door, the chair leg still clutched in my hand. Blood smears my fingers—his or mine, I don't know. Don't care.

The house is dim and quiet. I step back, shaking, every nerve screaming. The door holds. For now. I spin, scan the space for something, anything to brace the door. No dresser in sight, just the bookshelf—too heavy—and a few sagging chairs.

I grab the closest one and wedge it under the knob. Then another. I drag the coffee table over, tipping it on its side and jamming it against the doorframe, wedging its legs between the wall and the knob. It groans in protest but holds. But maybe it buys me a minute. Maybe two.

I fumble in my pocket and yank out my phone.

No signal. Not surprising. In the car, the GPS struggled the closer I got to the cabin. I hadn't thought to check my phone at the time, but between all the trees and the distance from town, it would have been the same result. But then it dawned on me. Theo texted me to lure me here in the first place. Which means…he had cell service.

He could have driven to town for that, but he's supposed to be dead. Would he risk being seen? Maybe. I think back through the night.

Every entryway blocked or sealed except the two he *wanted* open. My phone. My keys. The holes in cold earth.

No. This is the culmination of his plan. The part he's been craving, anticipating. He wouldn't leave anything to chance. He's using a signal jammer. He has to be.

Where would he hide it?

I dart into the kitchen. Pull open drawer after drawer—utensils, junk, towels, spices. Nothing.I crouch, rip open the cabinet beneath the sink. Cleaning supplies, rubber gloves, a bucket. I shove it all aside. Still nothing. Where would he hide something that important? Not obvious. Somewhere controlled.

I pivot and bolt down the hall, past the bathroom into the bedroom. I throw open the closet. Shoes. Stacked boxes. A folded blanket. I rip everything down, claw through it.

Panic tightens in my chest. Where is it, where is it, where the fuck is it—

Then I spot it—half-buried beneath the bed, behind a row of boots: a hard-sided case. Smaller than a shoebox. Matte black. Latches on both sides. I grab it and throw it onto the bed. Flip the clips. Open it. Inside: a sleek, rectangular device. No logos. One blinking red light. Thick antenna coiled beside it.

Got you.

I pick it up. It's heavier than I expected. There's no button. No switch. Just the blinking light and a flat panel on the underside.

Maybe I can just—

The door behind me rattles.

I grip the signal jammer. *Think. Think. How the hell do I turn it off?*

The bedroom door shudders again as I hear Theo break through my makeshift barrier. He doesn't call out, doesn't threaten. Why would he need to? The house is his, the night is his, and all I have is a broken piece of furniture and a box of stolen seconds.

I claw at the device, fingers slipping. If I don't get it off, if I don't get it off right now, I'm done. I'm—

A better idea crashes into me so hard I almost laugh. The corners of my mouth twitch, a wild, desperate relief. I drop the jammer and grab the chair leg with both hands. I raise it high and bring it down with everything I have. Once. Twice. The case cracks.

He knows where I am now. The bedroom door lurches inward.

"Open the door, Sloane."

His voice is calm. Like we're having a conversation. Like he's not hunting me. Like I'm not about to puke from the panic.

Think.

No. Don't think. Move.

I look around. Under the bed? No, he'll check that first. The closet? No light, no air. No fucking way.

My phone's still sitting on the bed. I grab it, hands slick with sweat. The screen lights up: *Searching for Signal.*

It doesn't matter. Even if I get through, what would I say? "Hi, I'm trapped in a cabin with my not-dead stalker-ex-boyfriend who may or may not have killed other women and has a fucking shrine to me in the back room"?

No one would make it here in time.

No one's coming.

I need out.

I glance at the window again. It's a single pane, old glass, probably original to the cabin. But I see now that the frame is warped, one corner painted shut, maybe. It'll take force to open, more force to get out. That means time. I don't have time.

I throw my shoulder into the dresser blocking the door. It screeches and crashes down, slamming against the doorframe.

He starts pounding, three quick blows that rattle the wood. The knob turns with each hit. The dresser shrieks against the floor. The adrenaline is already thinning, leaving me sour and shaky and lightheaded, like I could pass out just from the fear alone.

I turn to the closet. There's a rod—solid metal, not one of those flimsy plastic tension rods. I don't even pause. I just wrap my fingers around it and pull, but it resists my weight.

I brace one foot against the back wall of the closet and yank. The drywall gives with a violent crack. The end of the rod shears away from the bracket. Plaster flakes sting my face, my eyes, but I pull until the whole thing collapses into my arms.

My forearms scream from the effort. My shoulder aches from slamming into the dresser.

I don't think. I just go at the window. The first hit is loud. Too loud. It echoes through the room, maybe through the whole cabin. But the glass doesn't shatter. Just a crack, spreading like a lightning bolt across the pane.

I swing again. And again. My hands slip. The metal rod bounces off the frame and clips my wrist. I hiss through my teeth.

The fourth swing breaks through. It's not clean—the glass explodes in a storm of shards and jagged edges. I raise my arms to shield my face and feel the sting as slivers tear into my skin. One grazes my cheek. One slices into the meat of my palm.It hits me like ice water. I suck in a sharp breath.

"Shit, shit—"

I shove my hair out of my face with trembling hands, heart racing like a trapped animal.

Blood streaks my hands. My arms. I've cut myself, bad, but I don't have time to look. I wriggle through the opening, glass be damned. My jeans snag on the broken edges. I feel a new cut slice along my thigh. Warm blood spreads down the side of my leg.

My body wants to stop. Every nerve is begging me to stop.

I grit my teeth and haul myself through the window. My shoulders squeeze tight — the frame is narrower than I thought and I feel more glass slice into my sides as I push. I can't breathe. I can't think. My hips catch. For one terrible second I think I won't make it out.

But I shove. And then I'm falling.

* * *

I land wrong. My ankle twists. I cry out without meaning to. The ground is frozen, brittle with pine needles and frost, and it doesn't cushion a damn thing. I scramble up, half-crawling at first, then stumbling to my feet. My legs are shaking. My heart feels like it's going to crack my ribs open.

No time. No time.

The front door crashes open, and Theo barrels into the clearing, eyes wild, face red and raw in the cold. He lunges for me, and I stagger back, tripping over roots, lungs burning, ankle screaming.

We roll, tangled in mud and cold earth and pain. I manage to get my knees up, wedge them between us, and push with everything left in me. He goes flying, crashes into the firepit stones.

For a moment, he's stunned.

I don't waste it. I get up, stagger for the tree line. My legs are numb and barely working. I can't hear anything except the desperate pounding of my own heart.

He's almost on me, close enough that I can see the fury in his eyes, the blood from his split lip. There's nothing behind him—just darkness and the cabin and the broken window—and then he's gone. I hear his shout, a startled curse, then a sickening crash.

And I know. I know exactly what happened.

He fell into one of the holes. One of the holes he dug for me.

I don't stop to look. I stumble, half-running, half-limping, air slicing into my lungs like knives. I don't care how long it slows him down. I don't care how deep the hole is. I got out once, he could too.

The trees whip by in a blur. Branches rake lines down my cheek, catch on my jacket, pull at the edges of me like hands. Every shadow looks like him. Every snapping twig is his breath on my neck. I think I'm crying. Or maybe that's just the wind slicing tears out of my eyes. I run until the world starts to spin and my steps falter. Until the dark edges of the world creep in, threatening to swallow me again.

Not yet. I can't pass out yet.

My fingers dig into my palm, the pain sharp enough to cut through the dizziness. My ankle threatens to give.

Then, a miracle.

The phone vibrates, a single shiver in my hand. I look down. One bar.

Service. It's like a flare going off in my brain. A surge of raw, blinding hope.

But then the notifications hit.

Bzzz. One.

Bzzz. Two.

Bzzz-bzzz-bzzz. Dozens. It's like the world just remembered I exist.

Messages. Texts. Missed calls. Old voicemails. App alerts. Emails. Promotions. Instagram tags. A group chat from college lighting up out of nowhere.

I swipe up to open the phone and the flood gets worse. Push notifications pour in like a broken faucet.

No, no, no, no...

The screen freezes. Jumps. Then lags again.

I hit the call icon. My finger stabs out 9-1—

The phone jitters. Another missed call.

Shit...

Another fucking calendar reminder. A voicemail transcription box slides in from the top, blocking the keypad.

I scream—an actual scream—and shake the phone like I can rattle it into obedience.

Buzz buzz buzz. A Facebook memory. My own face, smiling.

"I DON'T NEED MY FUCKING FACEBOOK RIGHT NOW!!" I shriek into the trees, into the cold, into nothing. I try to clear them—but I'm running. I can barely see. My vision is starting to strobe. I trip, recover, keep going. They're stacking on top of each other, overlapping, choking the screen.

I swipe up, try to close everything. My hand slips. I almost drop the phone. I grab it again, clutch it like a lifeline.

Focus.

I stab the dial pad. It still lags—too many background processes.

"No no no no no—come on!"

My fingers are trembling so badly I can barely type. I manage to punch in 9-1-1.

The phone rings.

God, it actually rings.

"911, what is your emergency?"

"Sloane," I whisper. "My name's Sloane. I ran. I got out. Please, I need—"

A breath hitch. Too much air, not enough oxygen.

"He kept me—he said—he said I couldn't leave—he—"

My heel slips on wet earth. I hit my knee hard. The pain blooms hot and sharp, but I crawl forward on hands and knees until I can stand again.

The dispatcher's voice crackles in my ear, calm and far away. Location… injuries… stay with me…

The air feels thin. But ahead, the trees are breaking.

A gap in the woods.

Pavement.

"I think—I think I'm near the road—please—please—"

I sob, dragging my feet through gravel as I reach the edge. My vision tunnels.

"I'm here," I breathe. "I made it."

The phone slips from my fingers.

I go down hard.

The gravel digs into my hip, my shoulder, my face. I try to push myself back up, but my arm doesn't cooperate. I've lost too much blood.

In the distance: headlights. Maybe.

Or just the moon playing tricks on me again.

I blink.

I blink again.

Everything tilts.

And the world goes dark.

Chapter 10

The clock on the wall ticks like it's trying to stay awake. Or maybe that's just me. The cushion beneath me is too soft. The office smells like sage and printer paper.

It's been two months since the cabin. Long enough for the bruises to fade, for my ankle to stop swelling when I walk too far. Not long enough to forget.

Across from me, Dr. Lin reviews my file with the same careful neutrality she's held since day one.

"So," she says finally, "no more nightmares?"

I shake my head. "None."

After a few seconds, she taps her pen once against the side of her clipboard. Not impatient—rhythmic. A heartbeat she can control.

"I wake up around three, but I get back to sleep eventually," I add.

She nods once. "And the dreams?"

"They feel further away now."

"Do you still write them down?"

"No," I lie.

Her gaze flicks to me. Just briefly. She doesn't challenge it.

I shift in the chair, resting my ankle over one knee. It's supposed to make me look relaxed, or so I've read. I've started thinking of therapy like performance art. Give them the right combination of insight and restraint, and they'll sign the papers.

She flips a page on her clipboard, and I catch the corner of a report—hospital letterhead. I don't ask what it says. I already know.

"So," she says again, but softer this time. "Where are you with the cabin?"

A breath catches in my throat, but I keep my face still.

I want to ask, *What do you mean where am I? I was there. I know what I saw.*

But I also know what the reports said. That the structure was real, yes. That it matched the GPS from my phone. That I'd dragged myself out of the woods half-dead, barefoot and bleeding.

But also: that it was empty.

That there were no pictures. No belongings. No signs of anyone living there at all. Just four walls and silence.

I feel her eyes on me.

"I understand now," I say finally. "I understand what grief can do. I'd been isolated. I wasn't eating. I wasn't sleeping. I'd... built something out of the chaos."

"And you believe that's what happened?"

She says it gently, like she's asking me if I'm sure I locked my front door.

I keep my expression level. "Yes."

A long pause. She watches me like a sculptor checking for cracks.

I nod, letting it hang there. I don't flinch. I've learned to wear my agreement like armor.

"And you understand," she says, quietly now, "that what we believe isn't always about certainty. Sometimes it's about what lets us move forward."

I nod again.

She watches me a second longer, then flips to the last page of her notes, clicks her pen, and signs at the bottom.

"I'm clearing you to return to work," she says, offering me the paper. "With the understanding that we'll continue our sessions weekly."

"Of course," I say, taking the sheet. I don't look at it.

Dr. Lin rises with me, walking me to the door like always.

"Keep your circle small," she says. "Routines help. Structure."

"Right."

"And if the dreams come back, or—"

"I'll call you."

I step into the hall.

Outside the therapist's office, the city feels gentler than it did before. Not kinder, just softer around the edges. Like the world is still learning how to hold me.

I walk the long way home. Not because I want to, but because I can.

I pass a woman walking her dog, a boy carrying a violin case, an old man yelling at a mailbox. No one looks at me twice. No one knows what I've seen. That I bled on a forest floor while the man who loved me tried to erase me.

That I clawed my way back into a world that insists I imagined it.

When I reach my building, I pause before unlocking the door. My reflection stares back at me in the glass—thinner, darker-eyed, steadier.

I let myself in.

Inside, the lights are off. I leave them that way.

The apartment is clean. Spare. A few dishes drying by the sink, a single plant on the windowsill that somehow survived. And then, through the archway into the back room that used to be an office.

I flick on the lights, and the wall blooms into color—a grid of printouts, photos, handwritten notes. The faces of women, all of them tied together with thin red thread. Points on a timeline. Locations. Circumstances. Most are still missing. A few were found, bodies half-frozen, presumed to be hikers who got lost, accidents no one questioned hard enough.

I stand in front of the wall and let my eyes adjust. It's taken me two months to build. Two months of tracking dead links, cross-referencing aliases, digging into podcasts and comment threads and cold trail news blurbs.

In the center of the wall: Theo. Grainy, taken from a security cam still outside a rest stop in Kentucky. Not dead. Just good at vanishing.

My phone buzzes in my pocket, but I ignore it. I take a step back, taking in all the faces of these women. How many, I could only guess—there were only a few names I remembered from the IDs in the cabin. I wish now that I'd stashed them in a pocket or brought the box with me. My gaze settles on one picture in particular: auburn hair pulled back in a ponytail swinging behind her as she runs.

Evelyn Barnes.

It wasn't until later than I realized why I recognized the name. Years ago, Jessa and I were invited to a bachelorette party. Hiking in the Poconos. My nightmare. But the week prior, the bride's cousin went missing on one of the Appalachian trails not far from the guided tour's headquarters. The bachelorette party turned into a search party instead. Everyone but me. I faked sick and holed up in my house for a few days, but all I heard about for weeks was Evelyn.

Where is Evelyn?

To this day, no one knows.

But I do. She was the girl before me.

My phone vibrates again, a nudge to reply.

Unknown number: *She reminds me of you.*

A woman holds a coffee cup, standing near a stone fountain. Behind her, a bench with peeling green paint. String lights overhead. The exact town square where Theo took me on our "first date."

I stare at the photo until my jaw aches from clenching.

Then I move.

The bag's in the closet, buried behind old coats and shoes I haven't worn since before. I drag it out and unzip it, empty and waiting. I don't hesitate. Not this time.

Clothes. Boots. Flashlight. Cash. Maps. Burner phone. Evelyn's picture from the wall. I don't need it to remember her. But I want her with me anyway.

I pack like I already know where I'm going. Because I do. This isn't about chasing a ghost anymore. Because I know how this ends if no one stops him.

No one's looking. Not the cops. Not the feds. No one connects the dots because he erases the lines between them. But I see them now.

By the time I zip the bag shut, the sun is rising. The apartment glows faint pink and gold, all softness and lies. I glance around one last time. The plant on the windowsill. The dishes by the sink. The ghost of the girl I used to be.

I turn off the string lights. The wall goes dark.

Then I pick up the bag, sling it over my shoulder, and head for the door. This time, I'm not waiting for someone to save me. This time, I'm not running away.

This time, I'm the one hunting.

And he won't see me coming.